Efflux

Authored by : David Theiss

Cover Photo taken by :
In God We Rust Photography

New Commission Entry #45513

The following was found within a handwritten sheaf of paper left on the kitchen countertop of a two level suburban home in node 1803a

Also of note; a heavily decomposed and as yet unidentified body was found reclining in the living room chair.

This record is to be kept on file as the subject is considered fully developed into Roiler status.

This ranking is assigned via the New Commission. If subject Siridean Archer is detected, quarantine and rehabilitation measures are to be taken to ensure safety and compliance for the general population.

Chapter 1

Henry's dead. At some point that's only slipped into focus for a moment I know that it was by my own hand. I have to bite down on that.

I'm all out of squil.

We are going to have to keep moving. I can't keep her here, not when I know what it would mean if you found us. I realize by doing so I'm losing all chance to continue in perpetuity but as a severance I've recorded everything since the Resonance that I've been able to keep track of.

This is a peace offering on my life and hers. It's everything I can remember up to this point; the handful of memories that haven't been snaked out and passed on or churned up. Yours. Take them.

There won't be any reason to follow us.

You'll already have everything you need.

Chapter 2

I was working some shitty job at the time in a
warehouse where the hours were awful, the pay was
worse, and the only redeeming factor was the
amount of drink we managed to consume on the
company dime whenever we got together to
celebrate another milestone in the life that just
seemed to suck its way out of you. I can't remember
how we used to put up with it back in those days. The
feeling that maybe something might change if you
held on long enough, that maybe your chance was
coming up, maybe you should just hold still in case
something came knocking the moment after you
decided to bail. Whatever it was that kept us in place
so long was always expected to look away during
these parties and only check back in once we'd
blown off a little steam so it could prod us back into
line at the soul silent chopping block on Monday. It
was a christmas party this time, my supervisor Ken's
house. I'm sure it would have taken it's shot to drag
us all back again had it been given the chance,
though time and again, thinking back it seems to
have come down to the nasty little eyeshadow look in
Leanan's eye as she dragged me away from the
main room where I'd been sloughing cans of cheap
beer and telling stories to friends who'd been there
when they happened. Years together and I still
couldn't understood how she hadn't yet gotten tired of
me. She had something burning up in her that night
which seemed to cut through the freeze-frame jitter
blur I'd gotten past my liver, some kind of heat I could

feel through her clothes and mine without even touching. I could smell it on her, feel the heat rising pulling that thin little layer of off-spice sweat and scent from her skin out into the air and then the kick I felt in my stomach when it found it's way home.

I don't remember who was on top or who came first, who got who to make that first un-button, the first slow drag on the belt. What I do remember is the windowsill above Kens' bed. Cheap work and shitty peeling white paint, dusty windows streaking with the fog that built up between the cold air outside and the heat being put out by the writhing little spirit I managed to hold in place against my hips. She bucked so damn hard when she came that I probably still have bruises on my hipbone. When I managed to pull her head out from the crease of my neck to listen for the party, I realized that there had been nothing but silence past the door for some time.

Couldn't even hear the background of breathing, just a faraway murmur like the whole world was waiting on a penny to drop. Laughing something like a cough I pulled away from her half-bent with a single pant leg on as a flash of light came through the window and caught her hair drenched in sweat and the smile on her face, the way her teeth stuck out just a little past her lips and then darkness again. Just the afterimage of her watching me with a love I never thought I'd want fading from my short-term memory.

I lifted up my gaze to look up out the window as another big spark cracked white like lightning but rolling, tumbling, crooked for a moment and spreading out harmless.

"I think someone is doing fireworks outside Lean, get dressed, we gotta see them before it's over"

Rushing her clothes on as she's squinting at me like she knew I was telling a joke but getting the punch line wrong. She pulled on a loose black tank slid her panties back while standing up on her toes to look out the window.

"Oh my god! Where's my pants. Let's go"

And I remember that look in her eye as she's picking them up off the floor and despite the fact that I never would have gone down the roads I did and ignoring what it would change for the fate of the city; if someone told me it would be possible to send a message through time to this moment that my former self would pull from his back pocket and read by the light of the refracted glare of the end of days, I think I would.

On the principle of this moment alone, I would.

Plain white paper, hand-written, full page, crumpled and scorched as it passed back through the years and lacking any appreciable tact it would read

fuck fireworks

When the fire began to fade the question of who had died and who hadn't began to be answered. Once we regained the ability to take a proper look we started to notice the kind of choices the victims had made in life. A common theme between the ones left out alone to burn in the fields and in pathways around their homes, along bicycle routes and bridges and on mountaintops and in cottages. The places turned out not to be as important as you'd think. It wasn't localized in any meaningful way.

It was the loners, the elderly, the sick and the boring that got their homes burrowed out by the flames, rushing in cracked glass and turning fabric over on couches. Though the apocalypse only lasted about a week, the majority of the deaths occurred in the first few hours.

I've seen enough of the footage to come to that conclusion myself, some of the victims were in view of surveillance cameras. Some were filming themselves for their own reasons like this one guy in Argentina who had a camera on himself while masturbating to a video of barely clothed girls jumping around a volleyball net. The girls kept playing on screen as he fell to the ground hand cauterizing to his crotch in just under a second hair singed off at the eyebrows skin turned away from the bone as tinny theme music could be heard playing even after the camera lens had distorted from the heat stress.

Through it all he hadn't screamed or grimaced. I could even make out the start of a grin forming as the fire swirled in around him and I saw his arm moving just a smidgen faster before the muscle and tendon melted together and charred down to ash. In spite of myself I couldn't deny that there was something inspiring about his holding on despite the odds or outcome, the need to keep going inch by fucking inch, pulling himself forward for no real reason anyone could define.

From what some of my sources have told me the draw of these videos is that exact look in the eyes just before the fire hits. I never search this stuff out for the shock value, for the death scenes. When I started I could barely even make it to the last few seconds of the tape before it would click off and the bodies would be laying in piles of chunked ash. When you can see something start just behind the eyes, some kind of realization in every one of their faces before that Bic started flicking that they knew they were alone in the world and that they just didn't care. That they knew they had some better place to be or even some better place to try to be but they just couldn't bother to give enough of a fuck.

Those were the types that were all but wiped from the earth and it turned out they weren't much missed. Just a slight pressure release like a popcorn kernel you've had stuck in your teeth for two days that you've found a way to get out with the tip of your fingernail.

Just that slight release. That was all.

The general consensus directed at anyone who survived and made it back to the collective with that mindset intact was to just get out of dodge, get gone, go. Don't keep polluting the pool if you aren't going to swim.

And so the periphery around our kuhaugen city was reborn as a refuge town. I've been out to visit more than a few times, to collect stories, to talk to some of the old ones who made it through alive. It's bizarre how slim of a margin some of them survived by. Most are pretty badly injured. They don't talk too much about what it was like when heaven reached down to rip off their skin. They mostly nod and offer a big smile that reaches from one torn ear all the way down to the opposite cheek and offer you a little bit of what food they got tucked away in the back of their trailer as you ask direct questions to get back vague answers. They never build out too far from the city limits, just far enough to stay out of the established range of the kuhaugen. The New Commission. The self-established authority that has been binding the city away from anarchy.

This one old one Henry is a good contact. He's got his own place out in the community that they've re-established using modems and landlines, telephone calls and morse code flashes. They've all gone back to BBS days trying to capture some sense of identity;

alone in a big ring around the city, spaced out from each other like territorial dogs never venturing too far towards each other despite the incessant need each of them has to be a part of something again. Anything. Henry's found a way to get in good with most. They let him wander in now and then to their own trailers, sit and talk over a cup of coffee until he ties up his shoes and walks back out to his old blue dune buggy and motors on back home without dropping more than a few words once he's done sipping. Because something went different with him when everyone else got psychic. Or maybe he was something different before it all even started, maybe that's why he got burnt the least despite the story that he was sitting out on his porch alone in the open air on that december night.

I've never gotten more than a tickle while talking to him, nothing more than a little ruffle at the edges of my consciousness that maybe he's in there looking around when he re-tells the stories of the more defensively recluse to me in the privacy of the wooden shack he's built for himself.

The last time I was there he talked me into trying a tea he's been working on from these poisonous looking berries that grow up real close to his fence. We walk around back and look, and he's got that old man walk where he's in no damn rush to get anywhere and you feel compelled to slow down and match pace with him when he talks no matter what kind of hurry you might be in. He's wearing these dirty old overalls, blue jean denim, manure stains from who knows how long ago and a great red scar showing up the side of his neck that disappears under the african oiled skin he's wearing today stapled tight over one half his face.

"They ripe I think, They just about ripe by the looks of it" He says, and he's leaning down to pick a few and drop them in this tin can painted to look like a train, just big enough to hold a handful. They make a rattle ping noise when they land, he keeps dropping them in until it's about halfway full and he turns to catch me staring at the inscription he's got burnt into a piece of oak wood, all curlicues and splinters; hung above the back window. He holds on to my gaze until that same kind of ruffle skirts it's way through my thoughts like someone flipping through a book they've already read, pages turning faster than they should. Grabs a berry out of the tin to crush it between his fingers and sniffs the red mush juice that leaks out.

"Definitely ripe, it'll be a little tart, but you won't mind I think. I got some honey in the house that'll help"

Another finger full and the tin is full and he pulls himself up to walk past that oak panel without looking and opens up the back door to let me in.

The place isn't full of much, but it used to be a bit of a shock because most of the types out here live with so much nostalgia and hope that maybe the worthless things won't always be so worthless that they hold on to anything and everything they can find that might bring back an old memory when they need it most. He's got a framed photo on the corner of a freshly painted white coffee table with none of the faces matching up to his own but it's a beautiful family. Two little girls, blonde, matching pink dresses and a few years apart kneeling down in front of a sharply dressed african man and his wife who are posing with big open toothy smiles for the camera. Backdrop is one of those stock scenes of a fireplace and a couch, vaguely presidential look and plastic dinner waiting on the table behind to set the mood.

Every time I visit he has got a different family photo sitting on that table, in that same thin black frame. I make my way back into the kitchen where he's pounding up the berries into a little ceramic bowl flecked grey with constant scratches and use and he dumps the whole mash into a boiling kettle already going on the stove, stirring it up and pouring it all through a sieve to make ready for our talk.

"Good smell to em. Good berries, you won't be sorry Siridean. I haven't had a batch like this for a while that smelled so good"

Whatever it is they smell like usually I'm pleasantly surprised when I take a sip and he throws in a generous dollop of honey to take care of the tartness he warned me about. It's kind of like a crab apple jam all heated up and sweet and I'm not so much drinking it as chewing cause the sieve he was using has more and bigger holes in it than it should. I start to ask him about his day but he gets us talking about the new firewall systems he's installed in his computer to keep out all the hackers on the new war games that have been running out here in the periphery. He says he's increased the prize for getting into his own system to a cylinder of NOS, installation free of charge if the person has got a compatible car. Says he's got a lot of interest, but the majority of the attacks have been directed at a guy who's been growing his own opium poppies out in the camp. An ounce of opium hash to anybody who can get in makes for steep competition. Henry just smiles when he recounts the last bit.

"Fucking junkies man, don't feel pain right so they reckon they can't ever lose unless they want to"

Looks over the two steaming mugs of red berry tea at the presidential family beaming out at him from the frame on the coffee table.

"Maybe they have a point"

Something drains out of him and I take my cue to get moving. I go to leave out the back door stepping over a charred pair of shoes that don't look like anything Henry might wear, small blue velcro strap sneakers with little clear slots in the side like the kind that used to light up when you run and they look as fresh cleaned as they can be where it shows, pressed neat and lined up straight against the doorjamb.

Henry sipping at his tea when I turn around to latch

the door his head nods and my hand waves, and I go.

The people out here just don't handle the world the same way. Maybe it's just how they always dealt with their problems we just had no cause to notice their strife before, these types left up to government and police and locked up when they needed to be and kept out of sight. Few of them ever had any sort of home in the first place, not many of them want one now, want anybody probing around in their minds. Don't want to be a part of any understanding age, don't recognize the rights of anybody else to try.

The last attempted count of the survivors in the ring outside of kuhaugen city was at 726 souls.

And I know I've seen at least 50 fresh plots of upturned soil in the lot out back behind Henry's home since then.

I risk a look back at his oak sign as I walk to my car and the inscription it's got seems a bit more shaky, a little less sure of itself as I'm leaving.

There will be peace there

A shiver washes through me and I mark the lines and point my headlights towards the city sky keeping a close eye for any sort of shimmer and the tape track turns over playing Louis Armstrong on the car speakers with just a bit of pop that lets me know they've long since blown.

Chapter 4

Leanan's stepping outside into the cold air with nothing but a blank tank top and a scarf around her shoulders to stop the sweat from freezing into icicles on her skin.

When we left the room and creeped into where the party used to be what I see is the detritus of a rapture, jackets haphazard on the floor, drink cups still full of beer crowded onto tables around a tapped keg. We didn't catch on to it being strange just yet, staring and laughing all that fire in her blood beaming out from her face getting warm, tamped down. Her eyes finding a way to catch the light from every bulb in the room and coated dark in smeared mascara sitting above lips sucked half clean of strawberry chap. Confused grins meshing as we run out to the door and she grabs her scarf and we push our way out the door into the cold air.

A crowd in the street and it all starts to click. Some people holding hands and a few kneeling down in the road murmuring to themselves. Most still drinking in small clusters and I look over heads to see Kevin standing off with a few of the guys from work. He's cheering alone and pointing up at the sky as a set of sparks sets off one of those little puffball clouds directly above.

Leanan grabs on to my hand, I grab on back but my eyes are stuck to the cloud

Noise pours out around us, everyone is worked up and excited and scared and I can hear my heartbeat slowing in my chest as I watch the show. A feeling was building I hadn't ever felt. Something none of us had ever seen, or guessed or hoped or feared we'd see.

Lean pulls me close and I can tell she's scared; I try to figure out some kind of reassurance I can give her to let her know that everything is going to be okay.

"It's all starting to burn"

And I can't believe how soft my voice was, voices yelling edged with panic around me and that calm calm sound coming out from my throat had the same comforting edge that a serial killer might have before he sinks in the knife. She can hear it even with the cold shouting all around and the disconnect in her reaction is worse than I thought it could be. I'm watching more sparks spread out across the sky and something in her is hardened and shut down when the words come out and there isn't anything I can do about it. That's what I tell myself. But then she's pulling me back inside away from the crowd because she's cold and I can see Kevin's head spin around at me and raise his glass and yell hoarse with some kind of exclamation so I nod back before following Lean through the door.

We cross the threshold she sits down and looks at me and asks what I think, what I think is happening to the world outside but I don't know what to tell her. The lighting is flickering and set into the walls and the couch we're sitting on is torn and stained with spilt beer and I'm soft eyed at a pile of cigarette ends that are stuck in a crease between the pillows. I pull down, deep, reaching with any borrowed strength I can find to have a way to tell her not to be afraid of what's happening but there is a look in her eye that is scaring me and I realize that if I make one wrong word, say just the wrong thing right here that that last disconnect'll turn final. I realize her words have been bouncing around the room and I'm still staring at the ends in the couch.

I look up and she's been crying, my short term memory blips and I can hear what she's been saying on a sped up repeat, the tone, the pitch, the straining at the edges hold me kind of sound. I don't catch myself in time from saying the wrong thing, the wrong words and I'm trying to get the right feeling to bleed through but she doesn't can't see it.

"I don't know what's happening, I don't know what to do"

Doesn't see it like a mettle test, a pivot, the possibility that we'd all been waiting for without even realizing it

Doesn't see it and she's crying again just a moment faster than I can grab her and hold her and stop it from happening

Chapter 5

We began calling it the Resonance.

Had the half-ring of hope to it that convinced us it was going to be a good thing, that we would be able to endure it. As the effect built it became heralded as the New Age of Understanding. A godsend. It wasn't hard to believe when they said that it would bring us all closer together.

Chapter 6

Worldwide the heat is unbearable behind closed doors. In major cities, the tempest seems partially contained; unable to stay lit below cloud level for more than a minute at a time. Bursts of sparks are seen rolling through streets, parks and playgrounds have melted, slides and monkey bars warped. More than a few people are caught alone on the highway racing home with tires melting into the ground if traffic around them thins out for too long.

We'd just started to learn that with enough people around you the sky doesn't seem inclined to reach down and light you up like a burning bush. Convoys are thrown together, commuters trapped out in buttfuck nowhere gunning engines rigged with extra cooling and walkie talkies to stay close. The air temperature hovers around 45 degrees celcius as far away as the reports can come from but with enough luck, with a big enough convoy and the right rigged cooling you are told you can make it back home to your family in time for the expected rapture.

Not everyone is separated from the ones they love when it hits. And some of the memories have drifted in over the years that I still have a hold of. Locked inside their home for 34 hours and counting, the Smith family of North Carolina begins to notice something strange.

Virginia Smith, 17 is sitting at the fireplace, watching

the logs consume a rapturous silence despite the wishes of her mother who yells and begs but can't get her daughter to stop from feeding the flames. Virginia is too lost trying to push the thoughts out of her mind of the gruesome satellite cut video one of her friends from school had sent to her before the cell network had succumbed to interference. The victim had been out jogging with his dog in a city park. Carnival music rings tinny in accompaniment. It's one of the first recorded gunge videos to spread, and spread it does. There isn't much of a warning before he burns, just a few sparks. A ball comes down from the sky off to his side, directly ahead of the camera, before shredding apart a few hundred meters above him and igniting into the air. A tube of white hot flame offers no respite, no place to hide as the field of view is consumed and the screen turns white. It switches back to a satellite zoomed image of the burst, shows him moving somehow amidst the heat before it's gone and he's gone and the corpse pulls it's foot up, for one last bend and falls and he's not holding the leash for the collar anymore but it hangs frozen on a final frame.

Virginia Smith doesn't want to remember the hanging collar anymore. But she can't think of anything else, and her mother Elisha Smith, 43, is sitting in the kitchen drinking orange juice with ice cubes in it, getting overwhelmed by the checked white table cloth when the first flutter of *something* passes over her consciousness.

Virginia is looking down into that fireplace, worrying

about herself with a mothers concern.

Upstairs in the master bedroom. Daniel Smith, 39, is sitting on the edge of his bed, head in hands thinking about fireplaces, logs burning, orange juice and death, but he doesn't know why.

Sleeping in the crib next to him is little Eric, 0.7 and he's radiating this sort of calm, like a promise waiting to be made. Dreaming about things he's never seen, not judging, not worrying, not thinking about any of the things he's seeing in a way that makes them seem that bad, just seeing that they're life. Daniel looks up from the space between his white socked feet and to see Virginia and Elisha standing in the doorway.

And together they push all their worry down onto that babe and find a way to feel some type of stained peace about it.

Chapter 7

It comes out piecemeal, out of order. Even the memories I hold on to the tightest feel like they might have come from somebody else's head. It's possible that they have, the reins keep slipping around the shifting, spinning ball I got instead of a solid mind, and the squil supply is erratic which only makes it more difficult. Bits keep sloughing off and disappearing for days at a time before coming back just a little bit dried out. Sorting the fact from the fiction is draining enough; sorting your truth from somebody else's truth can be enough to drop you right to the floor.

When Leanan left the morning after that christmas party, she never gave me reason why or much warning of what she planned to do. When her crying stopped and I drove her home she didn't hint at the fact that'd she'd be gone the next day when I came back after picking up some supplies. Oil spot still on the driveway but her car was gone. She didn't leave a note. I used my key to look around after the flames had died down and that's where I answered the last landline call I ever got, from an officially consoling voice that asked if I was missing any loved ones because her car was found abandoned beside a railway tunnel just out of the city. One of the ones that sends a train headed out of town about twice a day. Went from standing in her hallway and to next to where her car was found in the space of a few hours, no memory in between. Char marks on the paint job and surrounding area.

I'm stepping out onto gravel feeling the stones slide around beneath my feet and the air still hasn't shaken the smell of ions and burnt flesh. The tunnel leads down, a quick tape job blocking it off saying CAUTION, and the words are pulling into my head as I step towards a car that has the big orange distorted butterfly X left behind by the emergency response crew.

The system they used was a code, a system for showing what to expect. Painted on houses and doorways it would appear on anything that a person caught alone might think they could hide in. Anything that showed recent occupation or an exceptional amount of scorching.

> In the top part of the X, the time and date from a few hours prior.

> The right hand side saying "Tank Full" letting me know she had fueled up before she left.

> A little "0" in the bottom part showing nobody was found inside, alive dead, or ash

I can't help but still look inside, I see the seatbelt still stuck un-reeled in like it always was. I see the four paperback novels that survived the flames; thrown as they were into the back seat. I check the crevices in the seats, looking for any piles of ash they might have missed that might be Leanan. I even sit down for a minute, stirring my fingers in the ashtray thinking about how maybe it might be her.

When I started walking down into the tunnel, I'm balancing on the warped steel tracks that line the way, ducking under caution tape, not even looking at the looming orange neon X locked inside a like colored box on the entrance, the sign they use to say it ain't safe to enter. Saying nobody ought to check cause the whole place might come down if I try.

I don't care. I've got this sick kind of satisfaction waiting and it's like when you rip open a christmas present sent by a grandmother who's passed away. Like if I don't go down that I'll never have to know what happened and I'll get to think the best but then I think maybe she got trapped in a crevice somewhere still waiting, running out of breath with stones all around, knowing if she just holds on a little longer I'll be there to dig her out. I keep getting that image in my mind strong enough to keep my eyes open and catch my breath short and I feel like rushing in but the logical part of my mind says No, keep your eyes on the ground keep looking for any piles of ash. One of them might have a little silver smear from the bracelet you gave her for her birthday last month. Keep checking cause if you end up seeing her on your way out the weight of that relief disappearing might make you drop down and never get back up.

There is a lot of ash in the tunnel. Nothing looks especially human sized. My flashlight keeps flickering like it doesn't want to show me anything and whenever it passes across the walls I see twisted metal spokes twinning out where there used to be pillars. Grey concrete melted and wrong where it should be arched.

I get part way down when the resonance effect grabs hold of me for the first time. It's like when you used to think about somebody too hard and they'd give you a call right then. Used to happen all the time as a coincidence and not even a week after the storm, it's being discussed by round tables of psychologists fighting with experts on quantum physics, both talking over each others heads about religion and out of body experiences. It was an early warning sign, an indicator; they agreed. People kicking up a gear towards the collective consciousness we all now enjoy. Down in that tunnel is my first real memory of getting hit with the effect hard. I had the smell of shampoo, an image of a stuffed brown teddy bear with half an ear torn out, followed by some *fucker* sticking his tongue out at me that's making me want to cry and go tell mom.

Not my mom, not even an image of who mom might be. My own had passed away almost 2 years prior but this was a very strong feeling that I should find her and tell her that *fucking* Anthony had stuck his tongue out at me again and serves him right I ran away from home right after. And then the sick little pleasure that he'd be facing the belt screaming apologies as Momma smacked him something good for doing it.

The thought disappeared.

Swinging the light around in a wide arc before it clicks off out of juice. The flicker comes back behind my eyes like a rolodex spinning fast under a strobe light and I get the idea that my dress might be stained. Hoping Mom won't notice that I fell in the mud so I can come out from where I'm hiding.

That time the feeling stuck and I start to realize there is a little girl lost and hiding out in the tunnels.

Her name is Amanda.

It took about 10 minutes to dig her out from under the platform, buried in a crevice that was piled up with stones. I walked out with her hand in hand, telling her how to deal with her brother, how it ain't right to be taking pleasure in the fact that he might get beat. Told her not to worry about her momma being mad about the dress. That she'd be too happy her little girl was alive. I could feel the words echo in and back out at me as she walked past the burnt out car all pigtails and tear stained cheeks and she looks over the blackened grass hill leading up to the nearby community of houses. Lets go of my hand and I can see she knows the way home from here but she waits around a minute kicking at stones before looking up at me with her shoulders set and her eyes steady.

I can see her lips moving but the words are jumbled as the rushing fire sound of her memories keeps playing over and over again until she waves and skips off back towards her mother and her brother and I light a cigarette with the thought that just as my flashlight was taking it's last lick at the darkness is when it showed the wall of rocks where the tunnel had caved in. Half a platform peaking out with ash piles lining the waiting area. She had been hiding underneath the lip, sitting and counting her breaths and thinking so hard that I found her little crouched form like a lit up beacon.

Chapter 8

The skyfire is still spreading after three straight days but it's slow and scattered. Vienna reports a continuous strike that's crossing along the tops of the alps, dipping down into the crevices and marmots are found dead ashed and flying rolling down into the Alpine foothills with the force of flares. A photo of one in mid-air still burning was shown on the front page of the Austrian Times website before the internet went down. No source is given. Body counts haven't even been attempted worldwide, few are venturing outside of their homes

With faces pressed against glass noone reports seeing much still burning except for the occasional cloud and it's like that only for a few more days. The radio plays nothing but static and the television is filled with images of scorched bodies transitioning harshly to marching military wrapped in fireproof gear and words from the UN that whoever is behind this atrocity, this attack against freedom, is going to be brought to justice.

No enemy is ever named in the years to follow. No reason is given. No mad scientists claims responsibility for the deed.

At the time, I couldn't have cared if I wanted to.

I'd locked myself in my 4'th floor apartment. Walking back and forth and trying my best to avoid looking at the pulled out drawers of the dresser in my room through the open door. The feeling like something might be changing for the better has left me, the manic hope edge caught and dropped in the course of a double sunrise is staring from the unmade bed. The bottle of whiskey on the table is half-empty and it isn't going to be enough. I find myself on the balcony, and the clouds are all gone, the sky tinged red and swirls of ash are being carried by thermal currents high above. The television keeps talking despite the ringing in my ears, and it's telling people to cover open windows with wet cloth to filter out the ash so we won't breathe it in. Reports of respiratory distress are reported. I can hear the occasional car motor past and the echo stays soft. It takes some time before whatever it was that brought me out here fades, but luckily I still have some whiskey left inside to draw me away from the edge.

Try to turn around and as I look towards my room a jet of heat washes over me, and I close my eyes thinking its time. After watching the pillars of fire reach down for days it seems entirely likely. I feel the turn of my eyelashes as they warp under the gush of air, but then it's gone.

It wasn't for me.

I open my eyes to see a scorch mark on the building across the way. The windows are broken out, the glass in heaps on the ground inside. The sign is burnt away, and I have an idle moment wondering what it used to say.

Who knows. The place is in cinders, whatever divination brought the wrath down over there instead of here seems to have made up its mind. I lock the door, tighten the bolts, close the curtains and look back at the living room table and see the crystal light reflecting from the facets of the bottle. The clock on the wall says half past four, and somehow the bottles gone down another half.

When I set it down again, I take care not to set it on the folded over tv guide with the crossword half penned in that she'd left behind the last time she was here.

Chapter 9

It's another mile or two before I get back into the city limits, louis has long since played out on the radio. The grass is growing back in most places along the highway though people are still scared to stay out here alone away from the core too long. The net. The web. The resonance. The back of the eyes tingle that's replaced computer systems and cell phones and hand written letters. It's something that would take a bit of getting used to under normal circumstances but when it's been forged in the hellfire of the apocalypse you learn to take this kind of thing in stride and count your blessings

Chapter 10

Dirty linoleum and off-brown walls, making my way over to the big branded coffee dispenser that must have arrived that morning, sitting big and heavy on the conference table in the basement of my apartment building. Some franchise had been making the rounds, risking the life of some poor employee to send these out to the people hiding indoors.

Fuel up for the Fight. Hot Coffee!

The slogans were shit, but the coffee was hot and I'm pulling on that little spout, listening to the spritz sound of the spout dropping coffee into my thermos. Bernard, the building manager spots me, he seen me as his ally since I stumbled drunk into the lobby last night and told him I was gunna fuck his wife, Marietta. He laughed deep, clapped me on the back, he was a fool. She'd been sleeping with everyone in the building since I'd moved in, and he'd seemed somehow oblivious throughout her affairs. But we started talking about what crap the National Guardsmen who'd stopped by that morning had said and some sort of bonding had apparently taken place.

"This whole thing had been predicted. The government had been working to stop it before it had happened but they'd run out of time. Something to do with sunspots, a flare of some kind. EM fields de and re-synchronizing, the burning wasn't really burning, it was more of a depolarization of the cells, and all that char and ash that was roaming the clouds was still sort of people, the same field disruption that had blown them apart was acting in a way to hold the individual signatures together. We may still be able to bring them all back."

I told Bernard it was all bullshit. Government doesn't, and hasn't ever known shit. They just have to say they saw it coming. It could have been pollution or something, and anyways, what did they have to say about why it was choosing to kill some people and not others, how come some people roll into town and don't have a damn scorch mark on them to prove it?

He had an answer to that too.

"Electro-Social Forced Resonation. Overdrive. Mental collapse shored up with an overactive thought process somehow produces just the right signature, keeps the fires at bay. It gets drawn to a certain wave pattern like a magnet, but gets pushed away by others"

I told him it was bullshit, said if he couldn't find me a scientist, he should just fuck off.

And now we meet again and he's telling me he found one, dragging a white haired old man by his button up green cardigan sweater vest who's already mid-sentence into explaining the whole thing.

(Benjamin Forsythe, 63. Apartment 2E. Resident for

15 years and employed for just as long working the EEG machines at the Our Lady of Mercy hospital just 3 blocks down, widowed 4 years ago. Had a cat named Jill and a fondness for vanilla pudding)

"Ain't telling ya that it's exactly what's happening, but I've been watching things shift and grow all the time I've worked there, even more up before the storm"

He's got a quick drawl that makes me think he's southern, not the type who'd have much conversation at work except for when he's handing over his reports and maintenance checks. A tech. Doesn't have the training to interpret what he's seeing, but it isn't stopping him from sharing the slow build-up of knowledge he's got from staring at the same wiggly lines over and over again, 9-5, 5 days a week for 15 years.

"It's like the ones that wanna speed up. Peoples waves are all looking the same lately, like they've all been trying to think the same way"

They probably do, I believe him. I tell him so. His yellow tinged eyes are looking at me, and I can feeling them zooming in on the spot of whiskey wet on the corner of my mouth, and I realize he's probably after my whiskey.

I tell him he's just been looking at the screens too long, but he shakes his head.

"Governments right boy. Those clouds are mighty pissed about something, they picking off all the people that aren't keeping up, its a very deliberate thinning of the herd"

Bernard is nervous all of a sudden, he'd been beaming proud when he brought me my scientist but a sharp nip of pain hits at my lobes and I squeeze my eyes shut as the image of his wife in ball gags and chains crosses through my mind and when I open them up his face has gone bright red.

Side effect of the resonance.

Benjamin Forsythe smiles at us both, grabbing a sprinkled donut from the large silver platter.

"Don't know any other way to say it, but I seen that too"

Grins big and he's gone. Me and Bernard stare at each other for just long enough to want to leave and as I'm turning back around to get into the elevator he calls out for me to come back, and I feel that nip again right up against my eye socket and fuck, I feel my thoughts slipping out into the cafeteria when I turn around to hit the button. I can feel the eyes of just about everybody in that room looking at me, Benjamin's looking away, Bernard's just scratching at the back of his head. Some old lady I've only ever met in passing is looking right at me in a floral dress and as the door is closing she speaks louder than I've ever heard any old lady speak.

"Siridean, it's been almost 3 weeks. She ain't coming home. You can't stay up there forever"

Chapter 11

Driving back into the city and the skyline is singed. Roads are still littered with burnt out wrecks. Sunsets coming and tinged that color red and it tightens up the pit of my stomach. The fact that the sun is still rising and setting seems like a betrayal. I start thinking about Henry in that godawful shack, out murdering folk cause he thinks he's doing something good. Keeping a family on his desk that ain't his and I realize not for the first time that the new age didn't bring anything with it but more shit, more loss, and as much as we keep saying it's a new age, there is no disguising the fact that we're slowly losing what it was that made us human.

Chapter 12

When squil came onto the market, about six months after the resonance took hold, I was sure to stock up on every cap the bathtub chemist in the suite next to me was able to churn up. The chemical composition is rumored to be based on MDMA, tweaked to run those empathetic centers of the brain into high gear, run em hot until the whole system caves in. It leaves the user incapable of broadcasting any memories or thoughts while in effect. The rush is pretty amazing, like all those signals are coming into a perfect kind of clarity, like it's going to give you some grand reveal, some meaning to the chorus of voices and laughter and tears and every time it comes on you wonder why you wanted to tune it out in the first place, cause it's all going to be fine once you learn to listen in a little better.

But then the rush fades, you get that blessed silence, the lack of an echo.

A great cosmic shush blowing in your ear.

The downside is a withdrawal effect that doesn't so much bother you as those around you. The detox spills out traumatic memories, leaves you broadcasting schizophrenic narration on everything and everyone around you. You become the derogatory voice in the back of any passerby's mind, reminding everyone around you of all their shortcomings, their weaknesses, their faults, pointing out their insecurities. Once you start, it becomes a type of moral obligation to keep taking more squil, else you start some poor soul who crosses your path on their way to become a Roiler.

The rumors that it'll burn you out completely with extended use are also to be kept in mind.

.

Chapter 13

Henry says he's been murdering easy since the day the sky fell. Set up in in his shack and he's never troubled by the amount of plots he digs. The people he buries and the lives he says he's freeing them from that they aren't appreciating right. I'm not sure if he was always like this, or if the resonance triggered something in him, or if came about just from bearing the raw knowledge that we still don't have any idea why any of this happened. But when he talks about the way each of his victims had some kind of burden you can hear the weight on him, that he feels he's carrying it for them now.

When asked directly he says he's just finishing up the work God started when he smeared all our minds together with a big flaming brush and except for the way he wears the skin of the last person he's met stapled tight around one half of his face; you'd never even guess at how insane he was by the sound of his voice when he says it.

He keeps the skin preserved pretty well, treats it with a chemical he shows me a store of, thick brown glass bottles; rows and rows. The masks do go bad after awhile, and so he'll peel it off, popping each staple out with a wince one by one. I've never seen him put on one, but whenever I show up on his doorstep and see the pucker of fresh skin, I look it over in every detail, each laugh line and wrinkle until he gives me a knowing look and a soft smile.

Because he figured out awhile ago why I'm studying it so hard.

Because once he waves me in, I'll glance at his coffee table and clench my fingers together hoping and not hoping that I'll see her face there. Because if I did, at least I'd know where she's gotten to.

Every time he catches me doing it, he just shakes his head like I don't understand.

Chapter 14

Leanan never had much of a family that I knew of. When the sky started burning and she left I couldn't be sure which way she'd go, where she'd run. I used to think there was something linking us before this all started, and that may have turned out not to be so naive. We've all gotten to learn a whole lot about human nature that was never known before. That all the psychology, all the medications and the hypnosis and the talk therapy and the Freud and the dream interpretations in the world didn't touch on the core nature of consciousness much better than we ever hoped it did. Edward Bernays seemed to have had it mostly right, people were influenced on an animal group level more than any other way. We developed language, facial expression, posture, pitch, timbre of voice, and a personal sense of fashion to try and impart some glimmer of understanding on what was going on beneath the surface. What frail bars wrapped, what a tight harness we force on the churning madness boiling at the center of every skull. If it wasn't for the resonance we'd never be able to have glimpsed at it in other people, let alone ourselves through the reflection. And that may have been for the best.

Because maybe it was that glimmer that sent her running.

I hope when she took off that night, wheels rolling on the asphalt out into gravel that she at least had some idea of where she wanted to go, some friend I never knew about, some old acquaintance that would take her in and offer shelter. I hope she didn't just take off out into the storm, turning her sights out to the city limits to watch the sky burn alone on the horizon with the same kind of cold shaken fear stuck in her stomach. Because when that happened to me I had to turn back.

The next morning after she left, I braved the flames and went to her home to see if she might be there waiting, to see if she might have just left and changed her mind and come right back. Even if she had been there I doubt I would have been able to see over my own hurt enough to take the step inside, but what I do remember is the sight of her window, blinds pulled back just a little like she might be in there peeking out. I remember how it didn't seem like an empty house but when I rang the doorbell. I could hear the sound bouncing off the walls inside, chimes chiming but no soft body absorbing any of that noise on it's way walking up to the front door to let me in.

So once I'd let the rush heat hope shake out of me I was able to turn my head and see the driveway standing empty, leaning over the little wrought iron railing with clear enough vision see the truth. That she wasn't home. Wasn't waiting. And it only took a few minutes to begin to convince myself that I didn't care.

It was the first time I completely unrelatedly decided that I had to leave too.

I didn't have anywhere to go but it didn't matter. I was
sure I'd figure it out. Getting back into the car and
starting up the engine, keeping a careful eye up on
the sky wondering about each scorch mark I'd see on
the path letting the motor run as the wheels pulled
me out onto the highway. When I turned on my radio
to break the silence I'd been stewing in the whole
ride up static caught at the air dirty little curls of silver
sound burning my ears. Click and twisting the dial up
until it hit the stoppers and finally I hear this one
voice cutting in and out but so solid amidst the in-
comprehensive squall.

Newsman calling out the end of the world, holding up
but leeching out just a little panic at the edges to let
us know we're all in this together.

So I click it back off cause he's talking old news that
isn't any good to me and I've got my foot to the pedal
heading out the first opposite direction from where I
think she is or might be. Hoping maybe she's got the
same idea and if I just get going fast enough maybe
the map'll flip, the highways'll line up in an Escher
like portrait of the apocalypse and we'll be facing off
each other at 150mph, gas guzzling tires squealing
sheet metal buckling in a head on collision of love
lost and torn and forced back together like the
universe could be a small child holding up two dolls
saying play nice kiss make up.

But it doesn't happen. It doesn't really get a chance
because when I feel my foot contact on the floor it

bounces off like it's burning hot but it's not. The sparks outside are leaving me alone but something is raging behind my temples and I can feel my hand clenching the handbrake and pulling up and spinning the car around as I drop a gear and do something awful to the transmission that leaves the rest of the ride home just a tinged echo of what I could have done. Could have been. Limping home on cracked and run down gears I sputter back into the city limits and thump my way down the road until the tires bounce off the curb and I'm parked back at home at an odd angle. get out. go into the air and for the first time notice just how damn hot it is because it's getting dark but it feels like noon.

Day two of the apocalypse.

Chapter 15

Her name was Cynthia and she's smiling out above the sheets and I've got her hand in mind and we're both pulling hard on the feeling of that contact to keep us in the room. My squil's run dry. I took the last hit of my supply just yesterday and I'm not sure how much of me she's getting through the dregs of it.

Apparently enough.

Flashes of what we were before the resonance muddled in with the moment, I can feel her nails digging in to the quick to keep me anchored. Room is lit up, bright, lamps on the bedside table and the walls splashed mostly pink with a bit of brown showing underneath where she wasn't too careful with the brush. My gaze and thoughts drifts away from her eyes as she closes them but it can only last a moment. She's back in my head, I'm there. Both of us are entirely ourselves with only the barest mental tether keeping us in touch with the group mind. Kuhaugen. New commission. Hap Claps. Whatever they call themselves they can't put anything in because we're both pushing out so hard there's no path to take.

I can't remember how I met her. With this kind of proximity her memories are coming through pretty clean and I pull on a thread that tells me this city isn't her home. Wasn't her home when the Resonance hit almost two years ago. She wasn't planning to stay long then, and isn't planning to stay much longer.

"Do we have to stop"

And the question burns, it pulls at something I thought had been drowned and there isn't an answer to the question I can give; she knows it as she asks. Neither of us has to answer it because this can't be about the victory, the solidarity. As the chemicals continue to leave my system I can feel that the new commission has grown too strong, far too large to hope to defeat and we have to realize it's not about that. It's about the last ember in the fire that's being puffed up to white hot and blinding and scalding the cheeks.

It can't be enough.

Not ever.

It's not supposed to be.

I feel her beneath me and my eyes are closed and the moment and movement has passed, the seep of the kuhaugen imprint starts its way in and then everything returns. The moments we can't take back come drifting out under my guard and I don't want to have to know which parts she's getting. But she glazes right into it and over it and she's on the edge of the bed pale and pulling a cigarette out from her pack with a chipped nail. There's a feeling building that I don't want to have to face and I think down to my jeans pocket on the floor where the last cap I had

had cracked and a bit of squil powder could probably be scraped out. I can almost feel it between my fingertips but then I see the smoke curling into the air, around houseplants and through the doorway as she hands it over for me to take a drag.

Window slides up and latches and she's sitting on the ledge wearing nothing but a look of smug awareness.

I don't know what to say, which fragmented thought to apologize for, hoping she hasn't got the parts that will hurt the most. Hoping her general confusion in life will lend itself to my aid and she will shake her head, look out the window, look back in and smile without having to ask why.

And she almost does. Rolling forward back onto the bed until we make contact and drown out the noise again, burning for some kind of sanity to share between us.

Chapter 16

It all just tumbles out in gashes. Little eddies of recognition and recollection and it isn't for the last time that I realize I've lost my mind.

Not that I can't find it, or at least recognize it when it swirls it's way back between my ears, coming back in through the resonance like a tributary trickling its way out into an ocean and then coming back through a cut in the earth, a stream I can remember as my own because it's got that flavor that I know too well. The few things I can hold on to all have that flavor, that same color. Everything else just feels alien and wrong.

First, and maybe second step to being a Roiler.

It's been about 5 years since I first met Henry, when I first started searching for the answer of what had happened to Leanan. The effect has been building for at least that long. In the beginning; when it was young, we were able to maintain some semblance of order. It was only the most vivid emotions, the most clear memories that could bleed through. It could be controlled. You could almost choose what you wanted other people to see, and we figured we'd be able to learn to control it completely as the years passed and incorporate it as another facet of our lives.

But we couldn't. The brain is adaptive, but it's still a

mish mash of the expression of hundreds of genes all meant to learn how to communicate and understand the world around us from a single perspective. Once you are forced to see that every other person around you is just as certain that what they are doing is right, once that certainty from a handful of different directions starts seeping into one mind, fracture becomes inevitable. Especially once the indecision and the chaos that somehow backs each of those certainties started coming through.

Year 4 :

I'd just returned from another visit out at Henry's. Most of the city infrastructure had fallen apart and the people tasked with maintaining what was left lived alone, in small pockets in subway tunnels and dugout homes. The circular camp around the city is almost entirely devoid of life by now. Henry's backyard had taken on city-like dimensions, pockmarked with neatly cut wooden crosses and stone monuments. He had begun making trips into the city, trying to pick out those he thought might be hiding from him, trying to grab anybody who was still hanging on to the old world, but there was an anonymity in the crowd now, identities shifting between people to such a degree that no one could maintain any sense of personal property. You could stay wherever you felt was home. You could stay until you remembered another bed, another doorway, another broken light switch and stained coffee maker that you could call your own. If you thought it was yours, it was as good as.

The Roilers had been congregating in the center of the city, those who had melted together just a little bit more than most. They could not hold onto any sense of identity, too many jigsaw pieces and clumps clotting their thinking process to function properly. It was best to stay away from that area. Anywhere they'd been or may be. It was infectious; the confusion. You'd see the occasional one out away from its den, just passing by, through the main streets ambling zombie-like and grinning and crying and staring like they knew you from somewhere. Always moving vaguely in the right direction towards the central park where a critical mass was forming that seemed to drag at them wherever they were. You'd feel one coming from a mile away like a distortion in the corner of your eye that you couldn't quite pin down, a pit of madness that would want to take you in with it if you didn't bear down and bite hard on your own name, your mother, your father, your favorite color and that one Thai meal you tried that you could never remember the name of. The song that played when you lost your virginity.

These things were becoming incredibly sacred. More than a few old friends were checked into the hospital tents run by florists, mathematicians, baristas, bakers, drywallers and politicians who'd come upon the proper training in the aether. Some of the patients had infected and gangrenous wounds from the messages they'd written in scratched flesh to themselves. That moment when they'd feel a memory slipping away out into the ocean-like emptiness, black coffee/1sugar replaced with caramel latte/extrafoam/nofat as their drink of choice. Like a riptide, crumbling out the sand beneath the solidity and authenticity of who they were. The terror remained visceral and would strike suddenly, even regarding the most non-essential of details about ones own life.

That's where I visited Bernard. He had scratched Marietta's name into his thigh early on with a nail file and the cuts were clean, healed, white scar tissue puckered in straight lines above a second and far too red swollen scrawl that proclaimed her discovered infidelity

"Kitchen knife. I guess it wasn't very sanitary"

He gestured at the wound again, the ointment still fresh and ineffective across it, the pus seeping out at the edges where it was trying to heal.

"Damn thing was still in the sink, hadn't been washed. Guess they'd been cutting up raw meat with it or something"

He laughed gruffly, and I looked away.

"Fucking bitch, eh? I kept getting those flashes, that she was screwing around on me, but I figured it was just my own paranoia ramping up; I let it be"

I'm staring at the wrinkled blue tarp that made up the walls of the place as he says it, looking at a homeless man sewing up an amputated finger with all the precision and confidence you'd expect from a prima donna surgeon. He noticed me staring, his hands still outstretched holding the stitch in one hand, needle in the other above the wound still strung through the unclosed flesh of the unconscious patient and he winked at me once before returning to his work.

"I mean, I did the right by her didn't I. I'm sure I did"

I didn't know what to tell him, but the bleed through of his memory of finding her is enough, he catches on to my unsettled need to console him, the tightrope shakes as I try to hide most of my pity. Try to catch myself before remembering my memory of first meeting her, but he's too lost in his own anguish to notice. I'm sure of it despite the wide forgiving grin he gives me, and the quiet lukewarm look in his dying blue eyes.

I can't help but feel a profound affection for the man. But I know I have to get out of here. Can't risk myself falling into the whole lost world of hurt he's got going on.

Even as he's calling after me and I keep forcing myself to walk away

"Siridean, hold on man..."

And I hear my feet busting the dirt apart beneath my

step, the grass long dead. I pull apart the blue tarp door and go outside into the sunlight seeing a lone Roiler walking past almost point blank ahead, turning his head like it's on a swivel to peer at something behind me. A slight shiver hits him and he bares his teeth and stumbles along home. I have to get out of the city, before I end up like this poor bastard. Or worse like Bernard, scratching at his flesh trying to hold on to the worst parts of who he's been.

I have to get out of the city. We've lost contact with most of the outside world but the lack of any kind of rescue effort suggests they're all just as fucked as we are here. And the storms that have been running like tornados, eddies of personality and torment skipping along the tops of the minds of everybody around like a stone over water, like a hot potato nobody wants to catch. If Leanan was still alive, I know I would have noticed her in one of them. I've visited other cities, gone searching, asking, hoping to catch some glimmer of the mind I remember but I've never had any luck.

I'm hoping Henry hasn't run out of victims and moved on as I realize I have to pay him one last visit before I head out.

It'll be a bit treacherous as the calling card of his victims has got to be coming out of my pores at this point.

I cross my fingers and hope that he's got a fresh enough face on before I head out

We'd gotten lost somewhere both skipping work on the same day, sunlight streaming through too many leaves and all I can smell is the fresh loam, torn bark and a last brush with her favorite perfume. We were broke. No money left, nowhere to think of to get enough to break even and nowhere we could really think to spend it if we could.

"Come on"

Not even running, but her hair catches the light and the air in a way that I can never understand.

I hear a shutter snap loud, iris closing, little bit of the light trickling in to impress as much of the moment as it can. Loud because she didn't even get very far ahead before she had to turn around to make sure I hadn't gotten lost. Or something like that. You never really know why somebody loves you, why they do the things they do. Why they hold on against all your flaws and want to make sure you see everything they do. It's a mutual weakness, an inability to see anything of value outside of your own little bubble. Dims the colours of anything that sparkles outside so it isn't able to seem so bright.

"Come on"

A little bit ahead and the path opens up into a clearing. You can see houses lining the ridge, city life and garbage cans and parked cars and well pruned trees and I catch her staring just a bit long at it. I can almost see the thoughts playing out that send her smile into a wrong turn and I have to hurry up to meet her because I know she can't see any part of that life without some kind of pain attached. Some kind of remembering I've never asked her to share that turns the whole suburban dream alien and wrong and sour and when I reach her I know it may already be too late. Somethings pulled out of the scene that keeps us both at bay. But then it only takes a truck going past that misses a shift to shake us out of it.

There's something brushing over her eye as I feel that moment evaporate and I get moving so she can follow. Lock of hair always sliding into these moments across her eye and I'm calling out to her and turning when she jumps up onto my back by surprise and hands me the camera and I snap one going back, looking at us both.

Sun's almost setting and I take her as far as we have to go and it isn't too hard because she's holding on tight and there's no sag to weigh me down.

Chapter 18

<u>Year 3</u>

<u>Gunge Video #439</u> : One Last Hit

I've tracked down one of the newest editions of the gunge circular and I've got it back to my place, loaded up into the player, locked in, queued up and clicking restless against the stopper on the cassette player holding the reel in place. The gunge videos relied on a method of tape trading going back to the live concert days of the grateful dead. Somewhere, someone was collecting the footage by hand and stitching together the physical film kinescoped from security monitors, hiding it away in some dark room somewhere, the soft white glow of a hundred camcorders all pointed onto the projection screen recording the same images, pulling all that awful fire of someones last moments into the belly of a hundred tiny mechanical beasts spitting out a hundred final products to share and spread into the world.

A friend of a friend of mine who'd spent some time away from the city had found this copy for me. Clicking's pushing at the headache I've got brewing, I've left it snapping at the bit too long and the images are getting too restless.

I've got a freshly open bottle of whiskey on the coffee

table, and that fucking crossword puzzle sitting still open next to it. 3 years unrustled. Even leaving town and I know somebodies been in here who's thinking they might be me, none of them has touched it. Someone left a glass on it along the way cause it's got a bit of a stain but that's all. The reel keeps clicking so I lean forward, hit the release, snap open the choke

It's fuzzy.

The screen starts out with a placard held out in front of the camcorder, it's angle held so that it can go into all the waiting watching eyes as close to equal as is possible. It's got a scrawled hand written message declaring the theme, a certain flavor of horror on the menu tonight. Hunger. Awesome. Awful. I don't know what the fuck to make of it, I don't really care. It takes just long enough for a long swig to burn down for the placard to drop, for the projector screen to start flickering and then the first thing I see is a man crouched over himself, curled down from the waist up with his legs spread out in front like he's just taken a shot to the stomach and slid down a wall. But he's still moving, he ain't dead; he's reaching over, grabbing at a bag, a spoon, a lighter. The dedication pouring out of his movements is all thats keeping him going as he dumps the bag into the spoon and starts it bubbling with a little heat. I can see a window in the corner of the room, mashed up with brown paper and tape and dirt that's trying to keep the sunlight out and it's starting to tinge just a little red as he sets down the spoon as easy as he can onto the floor and drags at his belt. The syringe is out, pulled from some unseen fold in his clothing. The belt is wrapped around his arm; I'm staring at the tip of the needle, the way he sets it down is catching the light at some fearsome angle from outside and it's got a red reflection going into the lens of whatever camera is pinned to the ceiling of this hellhole. Loaded up dragging at the stopper, pulling the murky fluid up into the chamber and I'm losing interest, whatever appeal there was to the scene is fading as the disappointment that this one isn't Leanan starts dragging the care out of me faster than he's pulling at the smack. I break away my gaze and notice that the bottle is still largely full and I reach to take a pull as I glance out of my own window, out at the clear blue sky. The taste of the whiskey still burns this early in the night, so I gulp a bit and I hope this'll be over soon because he's getting in that last hit and the needle is pushed in to the hilt of his arm, way too far, like he knows that the window is barking and snapping and I can see a rush of sparks push up against it as he steady's his hand to squeeze in that last little bit.

I don't know if the contents had time to travel up his vein and course it's way through his brain and trigger all those receptors. Don't even know if he would have cared, not for sure. Sometimes the fun is in the taking, not the rush. The comfort that you are doing something, anything, about the problem at hand. The memory that plagues you, or the pain that'll follow you down. But there is a moment of peace there that I hope he had, and as I'm staring at the bottle on the table, I can see the flames busting out that window from the corner of my eye and filling the room with a bright white light when the screen flickers to the next placard, the next failed attempt at meaning, the next hand-scrawled placard of the next sick fuck trying to justify his purpose in life.I just want the face to be of her so I can be done with this shit. I've reached that point, I swear it into the bottle with my numbed tongue and draw my line in the sand that after this video, after this next clip, I'm never watching one of these things again.

Because I'm not sure if it's consistent visual stream of death, or the way I feel each time I break that promise that's starting to get to me. Or just the fact that my squil has run low.

Because the whiskeys not doing its work to keep me inside my room anymore and by now almost the entire apartment complex is empty, and everyone has moved out of my floor to avoid the psychic fallout

Patio boards are old, waters gotten into the cracks and forced them apart so that they're bending at the edges and up from the nails, but still support my weight. Front door is ajar, I don't even risk a look around towards the back. I don't want to know how he's dealt with the increase of bodies. Idea's of bodies on top of bodies, buried in the same plots crowd out my thoughts and I start to wonder if it's coming from the man himself until I step inside and see him brewing some more tea humming alone into a calendar covered in x'ed out days.

It's some old ukranian tune like I've never heard before. There isn't any mask on his face. He turns to greet me and the words drift past unheard and I can see the glistening of the scars where the staples used to be. Years and years of them being stapled into place so that you'd think it would all be one big long clear stippled and white but some parts are still red, pink, fresh. He must have only stopped recently.

"Hey Siridean. How was the drive"

These words stick. Something terribly cold sits in the air between us but either of us will be damned if we acknowledge it. The sneakers are gone from beside the door, no idea where they must of have gone and as the question pushes into my thoughts the answer or something like an answer

Little boy wandering up to the front door. Doesn't know where his home is and doesn't know Henry. A quick flip through the boys mind and I know, that he's out here with a reclusive uncle but they went out foraging for food and never found any and so off went the uncle into the bush to catch a rabbit but never came back. Little boy saw the graveyard stretching out and didn't recognize it for danger, figured it means somebody must still live there unlike the empty camps that seem to spread out so far in every other direction so he turns towards it and hopes he'll get in sundown' -

Henry's mind whips out at me and it's like a glimpse into the resonance core the last time I ran out of squil. He's got more minds in there than a small town but they're all at peace somehow, happy. Knowing that they've been buried and that they'll be remembered was all they needed, the lack of the latter is what sent them to that pre-roiler edge in the first place. Hiding out from the core only exemplified that need.

I cough to cover up the silence waiting since he asked the question and tell him something about the weather, the road conditions, eyes locked onto each others and he doesn't give me any more followup. Both just waiting, circling around each other thoughts like dogs waiting to bite until he turns around to take the kettle off the heat and it comes through again.

-

Pushing open the door he sees Henry on the rocking chair, beaming out love at a photo of two women and a newborn babe in the brunettes arms, framed on the table that tips a bit on loose floorboard back and forth but doesn't fall when the boy is noticed. Henry doesn't have much habit with being startled and so doesn't know the motions. Kid's got the same kind of gift, they both realize it in an instant and they ruffle at each others minds for a minute until the little towhead breaks the silence with a smile and a jump and see's the sneakers all polished up and child-like waiting on the side of the door.

"You got a boy here?"

Asking with just a bit of strain, as much as any young kid can feel. Hasn't had anyone to play with except the dogs since his Uncle brought him out here after the fire.

Henry doesn't know how to answer, and the kid drops right down sitting on the floor and holds the flat of the singed shoes up against his own and gets to work untying his laces.

"You won't be using them, he's gone yeah? Not coming back?"

Henry still doesn't move, frozen somewhere back in memory.

He sits down in the kitchen, bringing just a single cup with him, looking me right in the eye and kicking a chair out from under the table towards me until it skitters to a stop against my leg. Pissed off about something but the resonance is only coming through in blips. Whatever's happened to him in my absence wasn't a total derailment. He hasn't gone Roiler, but he's not quite himself.

"Sit down Siridean"

I do. I look up over his shoulder to where his wood sign used to be, his mantra, his purpose, his redemption and it's gone. He's got a clock hanging there, old style cuckoo, the kind you wind up about once a week by pulling the weight down on a string from the base and it's getting pretty near the top.

"No, he's not coming back"

He's already got the set of shoes on and he runs up to Henry, shoulders back chin up and looks him in the eye.

"Why are you still here? There's noone around for miles"

And Henry doesn't know. Just a simple question and he just doesn't know why he's been doing it at all when the child asks. Tear stings out of one

eye looking out back through the windows at the tombstones reaching towards the horizon and again down at the picture frame on the table. Flitter runs through, first flick through his thoughts in nearly 7 years that says maybe he's done enough. Maybe all the works been done

And he pours his own cup of tea, running a finger over the edge after dropping in the spoon.

"Siridean. They've been reaching out farther. Scouts coming from the New Commission make up about a quarter of the graves out there now. They don't like ring city, want it gone. We interfere with the order every time that we have to go into the city to get supplies. Anyone who's gone in doesn't come back unless they're loaded up on squil. It's a stalemate that our bathtub chemists can't keep up with"

He isn't telling me anything I don't already know and maybe he knows it. I've been ducking them with the squil myself, on it for longer and longer periods, they won't hunt what they can't see. They've started to manifest the order as physical, not just existing in the space between our minds, they've got camps. Buildings. Statues of people I've never heard of springing up and people wearing uniforms dragging a type of solidity in their wake. Like a spotlight lighting you up when they pass, everything gets a little too bright when a scout goes past. If the chemicals in my body hit a low, or the purity is shit, I'll see them just for a second swivelling their head around to look at me, hyperbolic motions that don't line up with what's happening in the visual world. Beaming through the rice paper sheets of my thoughts until another rush dissolves the chemicals in my gut up into my blood and they lose track and I can move back into the shadows, an alley, anywhere they don't take much notice.

Quarantine zones are best avoided. They've begun corralling all the Roilers into park with their own kind, leave them thinking it was of their own volition.

The roilers disappearing from the streets in, the scouts in growing numbers.

Whoever started up the New Commission, whoever grabbed the reigns on the whole writhing mental mass of this city; they've got a plan that doesn't seem to far off from the plan any system of power has ever had. Control. Ownership. More agents. More scouts. More employees.

"I have an idea"

Eyebrows untrimmed and twisting at me

"I'm going to take them into the city. Each and every soul. Every one of them all at once as fucked up as they were the day I took them"

Tapping at his forehead and smiling in an incredibly unsettling way.

"See how they feel having to deal with this lot. I was doing them a favour you know. Keeping the streets clear, the resonance clean. Instead of repaying the respect and letting me stay out here, they just had to keep pushing. Had to keep trying to take me in. Don't realize what it would mean, don't realize how much I'd fuck up their day if they had me in the field. It isn't like they are prepared for this. They aren't"

He's far gone. If I had him pegged at the pre-roiler stage when I walked in it's only now that I'm realizing just how close to crossing over he is. How I picked a bad day to be in the blast radius. His pupils are vibrating with the strain of it, blurring into the whites, cuckoo clock ticking, pulling that weight up higher and higher until the clocks going to stop. Tick. Twitch. Tick. Twitch.

For nothing. For nobody. Of the kuhaugen scouts he's put down, he wonders if any of them were sent out here for him. If anybody in the city except his own scouts even knows why he's out here.

Little boy has got his shoes pulled on, laces tight, knotted and he's stomping them into the floor to set the fit. Starts wandering of his own volition and Henry goes to follow as he goes towards a back room that hasn't been cracked in over 5 years. Dust kicks up behind it as it drags across the floor and the sun is shining through a window in the back and the view of the graveyard is on

the other side of the house so neither of them see anything except field and trees in the distance and the clouds streaking through. An unmade bed is in the corner and a box full of toys is knocked over at the base of it.

Tick. Twitch. Tick. Twitch.

He's looking me in the eye and the connection breaks. Something else tries to kick up, something else tries to come through but it's mixed all up in too many minds, nothing but a smear and his bottom lips curls like he's trying to spit something out. A pain hits behind my eye, a flutter that's more like a water screw than a rolodex tearing up everything it's pushing through.

"Henry. I've got squil in the car that'll hold you. I'll be back in a minute, just keep that shit under control"

Pupils wrap around me and I push back from the table too hard, knocking it into a wobble and spilling the tea.

"Henry, sit tight man"

I turn around and break the gaze and start walking, can't look back. Hear the breathing and even the slop of the liquid in the cup and make it to the door, turn the handle, feel the air push across my face and through my hair. The car's only about twenty paces out.

Door creaks, patio catches a single stomp.

"Henry man, Siridean, I'll be right there"

It's pulling at me like a heartbreak, right across my face and twisting my gaze back towards the shack and I haven't made it to the car. Haven't turned the handle, haven't reached into the back seat, haven't grabbed the bag with my last few caps.

Don't have the time, storm pulling around us both.

No time to make it to the car and back before he blows.

Chapter 20

Melinda smiles out from beneath the sheets, gone after a momentary glance,disappearing into the folds with a mischievous squeak. I met her in the city walking home one night from a liquor store that had remained disturbingly undisturbed in the years since the burn. I'm dosed up to the eyeballs on Squil and it seems to be doing the trick to keep her from noticing any glaring misappropriation of thought. Somehow her ego is holding up against my complete disinterest and it makes me think she might be something special. I wonder sometimes if she'd even mind that I never think about her when she's gone.

Better not to take any chances and though the Squil can block out any resonance bleed on my end, Melinda's straight sober except for vodka she's been drinking from the bottle all night, and what I'm picking up on has me reach through the blanket to grab at her and send up a little matched excitement to echo around the room of wood slat brown walls and a bed dresser painted bright pink. I can't look at the paintings on the wall, don't want to let the scene sink in because I don't want this memory taken from me when I walk back out onto the street.

"Turn on the lamp" She says with a voice all pitch and tumble

I turn on the lamp.

The outline of her through the sheets hits me like a panic, seizes me to pull them back and I fall down on top of her, whisper into the fabric beneath her head

"And what exactly are you hiding from?"

I can feel her mouth stretching out into a big grin, eyes crinkling together with it, until she whispers back.

"The big drunk bastard who's wrapped around me at the moment"

And I start to laugh, just to hold on to one cut of peace in the midst of it all, just a little bit of solace in the fresh and the flash of it, but somethings tugging at me about the way she had to end that sentence. I bite my tongue, but it doesn't help. I clench down on something, somewhere that's begging me to just shut the fuck up but it's too late and the words come spilling out for no real reason at all.

"And what are you hiding from the rest of the time?"

Dropped and stuttered we both fall back to reality and the grin stays stretched out but there's no easy slack to it, totally forced. She doesn't speak right away. Just tilts her head slightly to the side like she's looking for a way out, but she's pinned down under my weight on the sheets, the question, the lack of sexual deflection. I feel her start to get impatient so I roll off, sit with my back leaning off the edge of the bed as she pulls her head out, blonde hair crowning and she sits up looking at me with a moment of disdain before the curve of her chin rolls down to her neck and turns to pull a cigarette from the bedside table. As she leans over to grab a match her shoulders follow suit slipping free of the sheets and she's just chickenskinning against the breeze coming from outside until she catches me staring at her breasts with a roll of her eyes.

"The fuck are you staring?"

Dry voice. She doesn't have any patience for my shit, but she's not asking me to leave just yet.

"I'm not hiding from anything"

The sound fires back off across the walls and pink dressers and around until it finds an echo somewhere inside her own soul. I catch a surge of irritation wrapped around a core of need, like maybe she might tell me what nerve I've hit but it's hard to tell through the mix of vodka and Squil.

She moves to grab another smoke.

"You want one?"

I do, I take the offer. I can feel the dopamine trickling down, locking into receptors to tamp down on the atmosphere of dissatisfaction in the room.

"What's your deal anyway? I never get the slightest feeling anyone is in the room with me, ya know, up here" Pointing at her forehead like I'm a defective with a slack jaw expression on her face.

I think about telling her the truth, in a silent private thought, echoless. I pull on the cigarette, and it's got a bitter tinge to it.

"That'd be from the squil"

The catch in her throat might be a laugh, a cough, I don't know.

"You fucking idiot, that shit is awful for you. You know it'll burn out your brain stem faster than a handful of meth. You're going to end up completely unable to resonate at all"

And she adds

"Dumbass"

"I got things I've seen, things I've searched out and found and wished I hadn't that I don't think anybody really should have to live through, even vicariously"

But she's too angry to listen.

"You and me both buddy, fuck em if they can't handle it. It's better to force it on them so that they got some kind of real view. You think you alone have the right to know these things, like you've got some special right to your shitty life? They're real aren't they, they happened?"

"Most of them, I think so" But the hesitation in my voice, the self-disqualification of what I'm saying comes through too bright

"Yeah, ok, so they happened. If the resonance is giving us all a chance to get a solid look at everyone else, if it's got any kind of purpose behind it at all, all you're going to accomplish by locking out your neurons from the whole world is a private little madness, a silence where we all got noise"

She's pulling at the cigarette now, hard little gasps angry and quick, the ember flares and sticks out too big on the tip.

"Self-indulgent little prick"

And flicks the smoke so hard it breaks apart mid-flight, loose tobacco falling to the floor alongside the filter and the red cherry spark busting up as it hits the ceiling, raining down on her bare leg sticking out over the edge of the bed. She doesn't even wince.

"Just go, for fucks sake"

I can't help but hesitate, cause as I'm reaching for my clothes and I look away and try to track down where it was I left my conviction I catch her staring at me with these big wide open eyes that are burning with a kind of hatred, a kind of hope, and nothing resembling attraction. She needs me to prove her wrong, but I'm leaving that alone without a doubt. She might be hiding from her own demons, but I'm hiding from mine and if the words tumble out I know that if I ask one more time what's sticking in her craw she's going to tell me and we'll both be left in an emotional limbo. Door is open in front of me, one hand on the knob.

"What are you hiding from Mel?"

Fuck.

I see the look catch again, she's staring at me and it's like an anchor. She's tearing apart at the seams doing everything she can not to say. Even through the squil, the vodka and the existential terror, she's begging me to stay and force the answer out of her.

To take a little bit of her own problems onto myself and make the world just a little bit more sane.

So I do, of course. And hope the squil holds out long enough to make it worth her while.

Chapter 21

Moon was too big all night.

Henry's house stuck in a loop behind my eyes too-clean sneakers framed family fear plots reaching out so far past his window and never to be dug again.

But I'm in a truck stop diner just past the city limits where some of the less damaged trek to from their camp's when the time alone gets to be too much and the transfer still occurs here but slower and I've heard they sneak some fucks variant of squil into the coffee but noone bothers at all at all at all to prove it waitress looks glares cringes at me when I walk in like just exactly like she looks at anybody else everybody walking and doesn't bat an eye at the blood caked into my fingernails and the state I'm in she doesn't care.

Points at a booth and I walk to it catching the sound of ella fitzgerald belting out 'misty' and it's coming out from a speaker next through to the till until her nametag reads Dorothy and she hands it to me my menu it's over and I'm looking at my hands again with more shock than she can muster

I don't know who's blood this is.

Wherever I've been it is safe to assume I've done something utterly final and whatever happened I can't face the truth of it now so I get a coffee grounds in the bottom of the cup to help with the jitter jeer and everything manages to get settled down a step to as I look out one of the few windows that hasn't been shattered broken out shards and wait on the sunrise I start to notice that the sky is glowing with a strange sort of light and I realize that the day is going to start out more beautiful than anything I've seen in a long time and the swirling grey it's forming from slowly shocks me into believing the truth of what I've done and what I'll do the world has long since ended its gone and I haven't said all I need to I make a promise to myself to keep my eyes fixed onto a window onto the window onto that pane of glass until it is time to go to keep my will dead locked licked on and ready to face the consequences despite the pressing weight of everything Henry's been and everything he's absorbed that I've only now noticed again again has been sitting behind my eyes like I forgot somehow.

If I haven't told you about the first morning I should have told you I may have told you when the day itself had gotten out of the night by the skin of its teeth when the sun rose tulip grew hidden away from me from behind the red glare it was strange how all I could see was the grass lit up as the clouds burned life twitch colors just behind the hills because now now now that the last stored final ray has long since dropped, skipping over the tops of this vicious gray sky like a stone on a lake, there isn't any place left for me to go that won't lead to a collision with the new commission, the self-proclaimed authority that won't allow any roilers back in but Henry had an answer to stop them and that thought is stuck in my head like a skipping record until a woman spinning in a dress without a spot on it hands that aren't mine grabbing her at the waist to stop her and kiss her and I see the love spilling out of her eyes until it starts turning red like it's blood and the whole cafe starts to go dark around the flow.

Panic spills out around me and I'm not the only one trying to pin down where this is coming from and I think maybe I've lost it lost the control and it's breaking down before I get there but there's a roiler in the joint and he's twisting out something awful and personal. I blink everyone does we are in the lockstep that'll lead us all to hell if we can't cut our way out Dorothy looks over the counter like it's me and I don't blame her with the way I look but I got enough awareness to make sure to shake my head. No. Not me.

Then I hear a sound I don't ever want to hear again, soft skull hitting something hard. See a man over in the corner on a bench in his seat looking far gone as hell and he can tell his forehead is dimpled but the napkin box corner he's rammed it into has met its match and it's too crumpled to be any use now but he's already committed and looking out at us with the worst noise coming from his mouth surge pushes through from him right through not a bit of and she's laying on the floor of the diner the girl from the memory laying naked and looking up with a smile and it doesn't take much more than that to tip the scales in back of out his favor

Dorothy comes up along the table with a pistol in her hand from underneath the counter and it's clean fresh pressed when he looks up at her and leans in. Wraps his lips around the barrel of the gun and bites down hard enough for his teeth to shatter in the seconds before it clicks and goes off taking the plate glass window behind him with it.

And we all only have to wait until a few minute later when everything everywhere goes back to the way it should.

Nevermore but that happens when your squil runs low and you've been out too long so many here just waiting to be put down but the memory of Henry's death, how his blood got on my hands and why it is there and the words he said and keeps saying couple with the feel of a fresh squil cap resting gently in my chest pocket to give me just a bit of peace.

The music has stopped but most of the other patrons have gone back to their food or otherwise delved into distraction, coffee poured up to the brim and on the house. I drink a cup and a half as I wait for the sun to pick itself so I'm able to get back on the road towards the city before my mind gives out under the weight of an entire graveyard full of souls.

Chapter 22

Leanan.

And the moment when she smiles and turns and her hair tumbles down and covers just the one eye. Fuck. The closet door part open in her bedroom. Sitting back on the bed, she's halfway through changing outfits and I can't keep my eyes off her lips. Her smile had been too rare lately and the sight of it is full like a lightbulb about to pop and I can feel my retina tightening around it. She's saying something but I'm not listening. She's turned around and then it's on repeat, her cheeks all bunching up under her eyes, white teeth filtered grey cause the last drag I took is lifting up out of my mouth slow and it's just the two of us in the room.

The window's filthy, but the bushes behind it are bright green and lit up.

I try to hold on to that memory as long as I can before it's gone again. A snippet out of what feels like an entire lifetime past.

It's only just barely enough.

Chapter 23

Somethings accelerating. I can't feel if my body is out where my body is, the last place I left it was in a heap on the floor up against my couch when I came back here from the diner. Flash of my whiskey bottle haphazardly slewn and spilt in a small puddle next to my head. I twist my fingers together and feel them sticky and flaking with Henry's blood. I tell myself to breathe in and I can smell the whiskey, wet against the wood oak floor but all I see is Golden Gate park. Venice channels. Skyscrapers in a city I've never seen. Japanese paper walls in a room with saki still steaming on the table.

Vacation memories. Hundreds of them are all pouring in between my eyelids and my pupils and it's starting to make some kind of sense if I can just get a handle on it. There's a pattern in the flicker, I know it. In the sudden jolting dreamscape as they flit across and it takes me until a dive off of the Niagara falls to realize I've been screaming.

Screaming and I can't move and I hear whispers of the Kuhaugen in the roar of the falls. The city dwellers. Those who live and breathe the pool must have heard me, and I find myself deciding without knowing how that maybe the transition wouldn't have been so hard if I hadn't have been dosed up on squil on and off for the last five years. But it's too late for that kind of regret now, they say it's okay.

Come inside! Dinners done!

Looking up from a pile of dolls, bicycles strewn
across the red dirt pathway leading into the green
grass park, smell of dinner fresh on the table rushing
into my thoughts, wiping down a dirty face in the
mirror, pigtails and red

**Just lift up your tongue, there it is. Just hold it in
place for a moment.**

A thermometer pushing up against my lips, comforter
tucked up to my chin and a cup full of chicken soup
sitting on the little tray resting over me with a bottle of
Buckley's next to it. Blonde hair, messy bouffant style
and a valium racked smile. A hand run along my
sweat-drenched hair telling me I was going to be just
fine. But it's not my mother.

Did you do this?

Teacher sitting at her desk, spectacles resting on the
tip of her nose staring at an essay with an A+
scrawled on it in red pen. The chalkboards wiped
clean, globe still spinning slightly where I'd tapped at
it waiting for her to answer her own question. She's
says it's amazing, says its fantastic, wants me to
apply for advanced studies.

But my reflection in the mirror is of a young child in
an oversized coat wrapped over hunched shoulders.

She likes you

Rushing fur and warmth and a wet tongue lapping at
my face, bounding joy of a golden retriever pouring in
and over my outstretched arms. Looking up and
seeing a familiar face smiling and encouraging me to
keep playing.

Mind passing the cream?

Grandmothers voice, motion of my hand sliding the
little decorated bowl across a lino topped table
towards her filling me with the peace of a duty done.
A tiny little achievement that I've done something
right. As I turn the hand over, and look at the creases
in the palm the fresh dirt caked into my fingernails the
lack of any calluses, it dawns on me.

This isn't my hand. It isn't even my grandmother.

Chapter 24

I have to get a grip. Whatever this is, it's trying to placate me; forcing memories on me to settle the inconsistency I've caused by implementing Henry's plan. The way he figured I would be able to trigger a self-preservation instinct in the higher-ups. That they might disconnect from the rest of the city if I went back home and opened the floodgates on what would pass over to me with his death. I held onto it all as loosely as I could, like a nuclear shadow on the backdrop of what I'd managed to preserve of myself. Everything that he became. The questions he could have answered, the ones he didn't. Forcing an unrest right into the core. But we were foolish. Over-confident. They could smell it on me as soon as I hit the city limits, waiting for me as I turned the knob on my apartment door so I could be somewhere comfortable when my last dose ran out and the floodgates could come down.

I don't know if this is what heaven is suppose to feel like, laying here immersed, but the voices of the kuhaugen keep whispering that this is how it would have been if I had just kicked the squil and dropped the inquiry sooner. That thought is like a sick that won't let go because they tell me everybody has had it, they show me every mind who's ever felt the same, but none of this is mine, none of this happened to me. If they're opening the gates to give me all the memories I never wanted, it occurs to me in a flash that I might as well use the opportunity to find the one I need.

I dig down, trying to remember what it was that got me here. I get back nothing but an angry dog bark, a snapping snake closing it's jaws an inch from my face, a city bus stopping just a moment short of smearing me along the sidewalk. A car burnt out at the opening of a tunnel.

THERE.

That one is mine. I know it is. I pull at it, trying to unravel it down to the thread, trying to pull at the sweater, all that wool and yarn burning off from around my thoughts.

A pile of windswept ash, sitting on a train platform. **Can't be real.**

Amanda's face, the little girl lost looking up at me and beaming and talking without a sound. **Real.**

Hundreds, hundreds upon hundreds of gunge videos; last moments. Lost souls, derelict bodies, addicts, patriarchs, matriarchs, uncles, aunts, hikers, hideouts, alleys, pathways, parks, homes, squats, hospitals, hallowed ground and hostels. **Real. All Real.**

Leanan's face smiling, turning her head, in that room with those bright green green bushes outside that stained window with her hair falling in just that way. **Real**

Bernard looking down at the infected wound he'd left in his own skin, begging me not to judge him for his own foolish trust. **Real.**

Leanan's face highlighted by the sparks outside coming through astained window, teeth biting at her lower lip looking down at me as the world only just starts ending. **Real.**

An ash pile sitting under a train platform, undisturbed but for a silver bracelet laying next to it like the one I picked out for her birthday.

Leanan's face dropping tears, looking into my eyes hoping I can understand the night before she left. **Real.**

Henry's face, stretched taut with the skin of his last victim, sitting in his easy chair beaming eyes full of love at the photo in the frame as the stove makes boiling over noises and a graveyard stretching out for almost ten miles glares back at me from behind him. **Disturbingly Real.**

Go.

I jerk awake; my left arm is numb, I can hear the noise it makes as it hits the glass bottle and causes it to skitter along the floor dripping the few remaining drops stuck inside. I'm already standing. This is all real.

Go

I grab ahold of the moment and take it in as I get outside to my car and start up the engine and the radio starts blaring blueberry hill by louis armstrong as I knock that poor old lumbering beast into gear and feel a hundred eyes watching me as I burn rubber, knock rocks, and motor down that road out again, one time again out to the highway. I'm all out of squil now, but it's alright, the road I'm on is deathly quiet. I check the time, check at a watch i don't have, take a glance at my face in the rear view mirror and realize that I'd been on that floor for months. Years maybe.

My nails are curled around the tips of my fingers.

My lips are chapped, cracked at the edges and leaking an ominous clear.

My skin is dry, pockmarked and sallow, tucked in around the cheekbones.

I've got a beard.

Chapter 25

Traveling towards the roiler park where I saw
Bernard last, along the way to the highway. He wasn't
doing so well the last time I was there, maybe he's
found a way to run the place like he always ran that
apartment building. Found a way past his whore wife
and pulled himself up by the bootstraps. Doesn't
seem too large a miracle to ask for after the hell the
rest of the world's been through.

I can't be sure it's actual memory showing me the
way or a bit of the Roiler edge starting its kick into my
consciousness. I find myself making an impulse
decision every intersection I come across that's
deciding every turn I take. There's a sign nailed to
most of the buildings I'm passing now, a warning
about what I'm approaching. Sight of a outline head
spilling out over the single line drawn shoulder. Roiler
territory

It's a nice gesture, but stupid. Noone comes here of
their own volition. I try to remember my favorite color,
nothing returns but a gap. Favorite movie? Nothing. A
flash of a smiling movie star and a darkened room.
I'm laughing and I don't even know whats funny
about it, doors are opening and closing on empty
rooms in my mind but I keep bearing down. If I can
keep them locked, hopefully nothing new will fill them
up and tell me I'm someone I'm not as I make my
way through. My knuckles are turning white around
the wheel, and as I approach the park I jump the curb

and roll through trees and pathways towards the wind flapped tents and tarps held up by whittled tree branches and rusted out metal spokes.

Conditions have taken a darker turn since the last time I was here. Whenever it was that was. Door catch clicks open, feet swung wide and out and the wind knocks the door closed almost immediately. I've found my way to the med tent where I saw Bernard last. I've got a bad feeling that is slowing my movements. I light a cigarette and throw away the pack, half-full. Smoke gets down to the bottom quarter and courage rushes in from somewhere so I flick the smoke away. Brushing aside the door flap I walk inside to

Cots are haphazardly stacked against the back wall, rotting food strewn around the floor along with medical dressings and used supplies. Syringes. Ampules. Antiseptic gels of varying consistencies. Bernard's coat is hanging from the post of one of the cots; still lined up perfect and all in a row. Most of them have white sheets gone yellow stretched up over the faces, the bodies. His cot doesn't have a sheet like that though, just a balled up mess pushed underneath his neck, and he's facing away from me.

"Bernard, fuck. Bernard, what happened?"

He doesn't answer.

"Why couldn't you let it go buddy, why did it have to stick so bad for you, what was it that got you here curled up like a babe and never leaving"

I catch myself laughing at the forced prose of my own speech. I'm surprised anythings coming out at all with the skin on the inside of my throat so dry it feels like its cracking open with each word.

But he still doesn't answer

"Some fucking gift eh? A great new age of understanding"

I swear I see him move. Shake his head slightly. He's dead though, the smell of the room doesn't have any hint of life in it. I take the unexpected hallucination as my cue to leave.

"Looks like the end of the world outside Bernard. For real this time. No majesty to it, no spark or struggle, just the layered death and quiet and slow crumble of the relics we've left behind."

But he still doesn't move. Just listens to the sound outside of the wind and the streets it passes over without remark.

Chapter 26

It's all highway ahead of me and I keep thinking back to the little girl, the subway tunnel. It's become glaringly obvious that I'm missing something from that memory. I'm terrified to go back unarmed, unprepared for what I might find out and despite the dread behind the movement I find myself taking the exit off the highway that leads to the tunnel. I see the side road leading to the neighborhood she walked off into, I've still got fragments of her memory, the path she'd walk home everyday from school. The map I'm following is like a slideshow set at 3 feet high, walking down the road, holding a balloon, kicking a stone. Every street corner I pass the more it feels like home.

She won't still be there.

I park, get out of my car. I'm leading myself up a side path between two houses and I run my hand along a green shrub about 50 feet long that I can remember having a hundred different hiding spots and cubby holes inside. Duck under a fence, I'm facing a back yard looking in on the kitchen through a sliding glass window, at a empty dinner table and a window half propped open by a tattered hardcover book.

It's quiet.

The whole damn city is quiet.

I still haven't seen a soul since leaving my apartment.

Chapter 27

"Siridean?"

Eyes opening on a bed cover, on a face cast in sunlight already fading.

"Lean, wake up, you're still asleep"

Those little lips curl up around the corner and she's smiling at me eyes closed without bothering to answer, just makes a face like I oughtta know better by now, and we're both going to lay there for a little while longer until she murmurs herself up.

"The day's practically already over, we haven't done a single thing all day"

"I know"

I try to feel guilty. I don't remember much, but it's a softer absence, asleep except for when one of us would wake up just long enough to listen to a song on the radio, or pull back the curtains to peek at the world outside as it ticked onwards and forwards without us. If the world had of ended back then, properly, not all these years of slow collapse, and instead sudden and angry, I doubt it could have found it's way through the walls into this room, past those shades and in through the window. We would have had no patience for it at all with it's heavy profundity and doomsday bullshit.

Chapter 28

Screen door snaps shut behind me, I can't hear anyone breathing when I pause. Maybe it's just some weird side effect of all the squil. Maybe they are all just rushing past me faster than I can see, maybe everybody else has just moved their way on to some new form of existence, transferring right into thought and energy and all that new age shit, except that the plants on the countertop are still alive, dew drops still sitting on the leaves where someone has been watering them. They look overgrown, lined up in a row along the edge and vine-like cords trailing down. The weight of the time I spent drifting and dying weighs down on me. It must have been years. Must have been. Because when I walk into the living room, looking over the couch I see an old body, cold and falling apart with a blanket tucked in under the chin.

Cared for enough to make me look away in shame.

Front door has the deadbolt turned, chain licked and locked. Footsteps above me on the second floor make me start. And then it's her.

I watch the shadows falling through the railings and hear the wisp noise of the dress and it's her, but it's been so long and she's older now. She's walking a bit more steady, with a little more grace, a little bit of innocence lost somehow along the way. She looks at me and I can't think of anything to say.

"Mister. Hello"

A thick pull comes down on my chest. I can't bear the mismatch of my thoughts and the reality in front of me.

"I'm glad you came, I've been having so much trouble keeping track of everything all on my own."

Whoever this girl was, she's no longer well.

"If only you'd come sooner I'm sure there wouldn't be such a mess"

And then reality snaps into focus. Her eyes are completely glazed over, skin is rubbed raw with years of constant scrubbing, scraping, washing. Something forcing at the back of her eyes trying to get its way out and I can't look into them, can't, won't, because I feel an old reflection coming through, the memories that were left in there when I found her down by the railway tunnel. Maybe she didn't understand it at the time because it must of lodged its way in like a brand, leaving only an abscess that couldn't heal, wouldn't heal, cause it didn't belong anywhere near her in the first place. She didn't have the tools to make it a part of her world.

She's on the stairwell right in front of me so I reach out and grab back the memories in a panic. Hands running through the ash, silver bracelet linking its way around my ring finger and dropping back making a little shockwave on the platform around me in the silence with a flashlight that's long flickered out.

And as I'm reaching in to take it away from her, the rest of her story starts filling into my skull

Amanda, hiding in the stone. Squeezed in when the sparks started racing through the tunnel, outrunning the wall of fire, holding on to the hand of the kind lady who saw her playing down by the tracks when the clouds above had starting catching. Lady said her name was Leanan and that she'd find her someplace safe to hide inside the tunnels. And the flash of that fire as it wrapped its way around Lean, a clean burn as the last stone was piled over a hasty crevasse tomb.

The kind lady burning up in front of her eyes leaving behind just a little pile of ash and a shiny old silver bracelet. And the image was all she had to comfort her in the dark, living on water dripping out from a storm drain until I showed up a few days later.

Showed up causing Amanda to try and share that thought with me, the sense memory echo of the kind lady's mind as it transferred to her with the airburst.

The way she died. What she was thinking as she did. The way it caused something hurt and angry in my own mind to lash it out back at a little girl.

Sealing it all up in her so I wouldn't have to cope.

So I could keep hanging on to hanging on.

-product-compliance

2659